# The New Adventures of
# MARY-KATE & ASHLEY ™

## The Case Of The
## Cheerleading Tattletale

# Look for more great books in
## ~The New Adventures of~
## MARY-KATE & ASHLEY™
### series:

# The Case Of The
## Cheerleading Tattletale

by Jacqueline Carroll

📖HarperEntertainment
*An Imprint of* HarperCollins*Publishers*

A PARACHUTE PRESS BOOK

**PARACHUTE PRESS**

Parachute Publishing, L.L.C.
156 Fifth Avenue
New York, NY 10010

**DUALSTAR PUBLICATIONS**

Dualstar Publications
1801 Century Park East
12th Floor
Los Angeles, CA 90067

## HarperEntertainment

*An Imprint of* HarperCollins*Publishers*
10 East 53rd Street, New York, NY 10022

For information address HarperCollins Publishers Inc.,
10 East 53rd Street, New York, NY 10022.

ISBN 0-06-059512-4

First printing: July 2004

Printed in the United States of America

## www.mary-kateandashley.com

10 9 8 7 6 5 4 3 2 1

# 1

# LET'S GO, EAGLES!

*"The Eagles are at it again!*
*We're flying so high!*
*We'll touch the sky!*
*The Eagles are here to win!"*

I bent my knees and jumped as high as I could into a toe touch. The six other cheerleaders on my squad jumped too. We landed and raised our arms in a high *V*. "Go, Eagles!" we shouted together.

"That was great!" Our coach, Shannon Shelby, gave us a thumbs-up.

Shannon is a CIT—a coach-in-training—here at Camp Pom-Pom. She's fifteen, with short blond hair and huge dimples in her cheeks.

"You're totally ready for the Cheerlympics!" she said.

The Cheerlympics is a contest between the best squad from our camp and the best from Camp Spirit, another camp a few miles away. And this summer our squad, the Eagles, is going to face the Pirates from Camp Spirit. I can't wait!

"Camp Pom-Pom rocks!" I said to my sister, Ashley. I spun around on the big grassy square in the middle of Orange Grove College, where camp is held. This was our second summer at Camp Pom-Pom.

"I know!" Ashley said, giving me a high five. "It's so much fun to be back, Mary-Kate!"

"Here come our buses," Shannon said, pointing to the road leading into camp.

My heart thumped as I watched the two

big orange buses drive up. After a whole week of learning splits, jumps, and even an awesome Pyramid, it was almost time for the Cheerlympics to start!

The second week of camp was going to be all about the Cheerlympics. There are four contests—Best Cheer, Best Spirit, Best Stunt, and Best Dance. Today we were doing Best Cheer.

"Look out, Pirates!" Ashley cried, shaking her purple-and-yellow pom-poms. Her strawberry-blond ponytail bounced. "The Eagles are on the way!"

"Go, Eagles!" we all yelled as we grabbed our gym bags and raced to the buses. The other Camp Pom-Pom squads—the Tigers, Bears, Dragons, and Sharks—ran to get on the bus too. So did the other coaches and Ms. Braun, the camp director.

I sat down next to Ashley on the bus. "My stomach is doing cartwheels—and back handsprings too," I said.

Risa Alvarez shook her purple-and-yellow pom-poms. "There's nothing to worry about," she declared. "Ashley's cheer is great!" She took a seat across the aisle from us. "She's a perfect captain!"

Ashley blushed and smiled. "Thanks," she said.

When our squad voted for captain, Ashley won! She leads the cheers and helps Shannon coach. And she wrote the cheer we're doing today—words, moves, everything!

"I'm glad all the squads from Camp Pom-Pom are coming to cheer us on," Ashley said as the bus pulled away from camp.

"Guess who else will be there to root for you," Kayla Majors said from the seat in front of me. Kayla is ten years old like the rest of us, and has bright red hair. She's captain of the Bears.

"Who?" Jessica Kim asked. She was sitting next to Kayla, reading a letter.

Kayla giggled and held up a picture cut from a magazine. "Justin DiNardo."

Everyone laughed. Kayla is a total DiNardo fan. She has a zillion pictures of the teen movie star taped to the walls of her dorm room.

Kayla's green eyes sparkled. "After the contest I'm going to give this picture to my stepsister, Tara."

"Oh, right," Ashley said. "Tara goes to Camp Spirit."

Kayla nodded. "She's crazy about Justin too."

"Oh, wow, I just remembered. Tara's on the Pirates," I said. "Is she excited about the Cheerlympics?"

"You bet," Kayla said. "She told me that Patty O'Leary came up with totally great cheers and routines. Patty's positive they're going to win the whole Cheerlympics."

Ashley and I smiled at each other.

Patty O'Leary is captain of the Pirates at

Camp Spirit. At home she is our next-door neighbor. Sometimes we call her *Princess* Patty because she's so spoiled. She wants to be number one in everything.

"We're going to prove that Patty is wrong," I declared. "Right?"

"Go, Eagles!" everyone cheered.

Our bus pulled into Camp Spirit's long driveway. On one side were big brick dorm buildings and an Olympic-size gym. On the other side was the practice field.

"Those must be the Pirates," Ashley said. She pointed to a group of girls in red cheerleading uniforms. They were doing warm-up exercises on the field.

My stomach did a *double* back hand-spring! It was almost time for the contest!

When we got off the bus, the other Camp Pom-Pom squads went to sit in the bleachers. We ran onto the field and began our warm-up stretches.

I waved at Patty but she didn't see me.

She and the Pirates were getting ready to practice their cheer. I watched them as I did my leg stretches.

The Pirates divided into two groups. Then they did running cartwheels toward each other.

I stopped stretching and stared.

*That's weird*, I thought. *Our cheer starts the exact same way.*

The Pirates cartwheeled into a straight line and stopped.

*If they jump into a split*, I thought, *it will be* really *weird.*

The Pirates jumped into a split. Then they leaped up and put their hands on their hips.

"Did you see that?" Christy Taylor cried. "That's exactly what *we* do."

"I know!" I said, my mouth dropping open. "I don't believe it!"

Ashley was facing the other way. "Come on, Mary-Kate, don't think about the Pirates. We have to warm up."

"Ashley, I think you should watch this," I said.

"*Go! Pirates! Win!*" Patty and her squad shouted. "*The Pirates are at it again!*"

"Whoa!" Shannon said. "Those are the words to *our* cheer!"

Our whole squad stared at the Pirates.

"*We're sailing so far!*" The Pirates stuck their right arms up in the air. "*We'll touch the stars!*" The Pirates put their left arms up.

"They're doing the same moves!" Risa cried.

"*The Pirates are here to win!*" Patty and the Pirates leaped into a toe touch. They landed and raised their arms in a high *V*. "Go, Pirates!" they yelled.

"I don't believe it!" I cried again. "The Pirates stole our cheer!"

## WHO STOLE THE CHEER?

"**M**ary-Kate's right!" Jenna Riley declared. "That was *our* cheer."

"Move for move! Word for word!" I said. "All they did was change *flying* to *sailing* and *sky* to *stars*!"

At that moment a woman's voice came over the loudspeaker. "Attention, everyone!"

We all looked toward the judging stand in front of the bleachers. A young woman with long dark hair sat behind the microphone. Two women sat next to her.

"Those are the judges," Shannon told us. "They're all cheerleading coaches at the state university."

"It's time for the coin toss to see which squad will cheer first today," the dark-haired judge announced. "Captains, please call heads or tails."

"Heads!" Patty shouted as the judge flipped a quarter into the air.

"Tails!" said Ashley.

"Cross your fingers for tails!" I said to Ashley. "If we go first, the Pirates can't do our cheer!"

"Heads it is!" the judge declared. "The Pirates will go first in the Best Cheer contest!"

"Oh, no." I groaned.

"What are we going to do now?" cried Jessica. "We can't do the same cheer after them!"

14

"What else *can* we do?" Risa asked.

"I know!" Ashley said quickly. "We can do 'Eagles Soar.'"

"Good thinking, Ashley," Shannon said.

"We haven't practiced that one since last week!" Jessica argued. "We should do 'Who Are We Cheering For?' It's easier."

"'Eagles Soar' has more moves," Shannon said. "And it's much more fun. We can do it!"

At that moment the dark-haired judge blew her whistle. The Best Cheer contest was starting!

Patty and the Pirates cartwheeled onto the field and started their cheer.

"Go Pirates!" The other squads from Camp Spirit whooped and hollered in the bleachers.

"They're really good," Nicole Watson said, twisting a pigtail around her finger.

"Sure—because they stole our cheer," I declared.

"I thought so too at first, Mary-Kate," Shannon told me. "Now I'm not so sure."

"But it's exactly like the one Ashley wrote!" I said as the Pirates jumped into a perfect split.

Shannon nodded. "But remember, everybody in cheerleading uses those moves."

"A lot of cheers have the same words too," Ashley added.

"That's true," I admitted. Ashley is very logical. Sometimes I jump to conclusions. "But don't you think it's weird that they are *so* much alike?"

"It's very weird," Ashley agreed.

The Pirates finished their cheer and ran off the field. The Camp Spirit crowd cheered wildly.

Now it was our turn. Shannon gave us a quick pep talk. "Remember—point your toes, keep your backs straight, and, most important, have tons of fun! That's what cheering is all about!"

"Let's go, Eagles!" we shouted. We ran onto the field. The Camp Pom-Pom crowd clapped and yelled.

"*Eagles fly!*" we cheered. We waved our purple-and-yellow pom-poms in a circle over our heads. "*Eagles soar! The Eagles are back and better than before!*"

We dropped our pom-poms in front of us. *So far, so good!* I thought. I concentrated on remembering the rest of the words and moves.

Everybody jumped up and landed in a split. Nicole stumbled a little as she leaped to her feet. And Christy dropped a pom-pom. But they both recovered really fast.

"*Eagles fly, Eagles soar!*" we cheered, shaking our pom-poms in the air. "*Purple and yellow are winners once more!*"

The last move was a spread eagle. It's like a toe touch but not as high. We all did the spread eagle and ran off the field together. *Yes!* I thought. *We did it!*

Shannon gave us all hugs. "That was excellent! I knew you could do it!"

"Our spread eagle was a mess," Jessica grumbled. "We didn't jump at the same time. I knew that would happen! If I were captain, I would have picked 'Who Are We Cheering For?'"

I rolled my eyes. Jessica wanted to be captain of the Eagles, but the squad voted for Ashley. Now she always finds something wrong with what Ashley does!

"Attention, everyone!" the dark-haired judge's voice boomed out.

"This is it!" I whispered. I grabbed Ashley's hand.

"It was very close," the judge declared. "The Eagles from Camp Pom-Pom got eight out of ten points!"

I held my breath.

"And for the Pirates of Camp Spirit—nine points!" the judge said. "The Pirates have won the Best Cheer contest!"

We were disappointed, but we all clapped anyway. The Pirates and their crowd jumped up and down and screamed. Kayla Majors ran onto the field and hugged her stepsister, Tara.

Patty ran toward us.

"Uh-oh," I whispered to Ashley. "Get ready for some bragging."

"Hi, Mary-Kate! Hi, Ashley!" Patty said. "We won!" She had a huge smile on her face.

"Congratulations, Patty," Ashley and I both said.

Patty beamed. "Thanks! I knew we'd win. Our squad has the best captain—me! I wrote the most awesome cheer."

"Now you have some really good news to write home about," Shannon said.

Patty laughed. "I'm done with writing for now," she said. "I'm going to call home. I'll be sure to tell my parents you tried your best but came in second." She tossed her brown ponytail and ran back to the Pirates.

Ashley and I both stared after her, then shook our heads. Patty always looked for ways to be better than us.

Jessica frowned. "I knew we should have practiced *all* our cheers instead of just the one Ashley wrote. We would have been better prepared."

"That's not fair," I said. "It's not Ashley's fault that the Pirates came up with the same thing."

"And wait until the Pirates see our Spirit cheer when they come to Camp Pom-Pom tomorrow," Ashley reminded everybody. "It's totally one of a kind!"

"It's time for the second contest in the Cheerlympics—the Best Spirit contest!" Ms. Braun, our camp director, announced to the crowd the next day. She used to be a cheerleader, and she's tall and thin, with short brown hair.

I stood at the edge of Camp Pom-Pom's

field with the rest of the Eagles. We all wore drums around our necks. "These drums will really pump up the crowd!" I said to Ashley.

Ashley nodded. "I can't wait! I totally love this cheer!"

A Spirit cheer is special because you can use all kinds of props, like funny hats or balloons, to get the crowd excited.

"I'm glad the Pirates are going first again," I said. They had already won the coin toss. "This time, the best gets saved for last!" I laughed.

The same dark-haired judge from the day before came to the microphone. "Pirates, please begin!"

*Boom! Boom! Boom!* The Pirates came around the bleachers and marched onto the field.

Ashley gasped.

Shannon stared.

My mouth dropped open.

"They're wearing drums!" I exclaimed.

*Boom! Boom! Boom!* The Pirates stopped marching and started cheering.

*"Can you hear the beat?*
*Start clapping!*
*Can you feel the beat?*
*Start stamping!"*

"Drums, words—it's the same as ours!" I said.

"And look what they're doing now, Mary-Kate!" Ashley cried.

One of the Pirates kept pounding her drum. The others took theirs off. They did a back handspring, then a forward handspring.

"They're doing *our* cheer!" I said. "Again!"

*"Clap your hands and stamp your feet!*
*When it comes to spirit,*
*The Pirates can't be beat!"*

The Pirates put their drums back on and marched off the field. *Boom! Boom! Boom!*

"What are we going to do?" Risa cried.

"We don't have a backup Spirit cheer!"

"Get rid of the drums," Shannon said quickly. "Just clap your hands over your heads. And instead of the handsprings, do cartwheels in a circle."

"We can do the last four lines first," Ashley said.

"And the first four lines second—that's good!" Shannon agreed. "Start with '*Clap your hands and stamp your feet.*' Everybody got that?"

"Got it!" I said. "I hope!"

"Have fun, and you'll be great!" Shannon promised.

"Next up, Camp Pom-Pom's Eagles!" the judge announced.

I dropped my drum and ran onto the field with the squad. *Concentrate!* I told myself. *Forget about the Pirates for now! Remember what Shannon always says— have fun!*

"*Clap your hands and stamp your feet!*" I

shouted and clapped as we marched. *"When it comes to spirit, the Eagles can't be beat!"*

We stopped marching. What was next? I didn't remember! And I could tell the others didn't either!

"Cartwheels in a circle!" Ashley whispered loudly. "To the right, then the left!"

We did our cartwheels. We shouted the rest of the cheer and marched off the field clapping our hands.

It didn't take the judges long to pick the winner. Eagles—five points. Pirates—eight. The Camp Spirit fans screamed and clapped. Our whole squad looked upset.

"Someone is stealing our cheers," Ashley said. "But who?"

"And how?" I added.

"I'm going tell Ms. Braun!" Shannon declared.

"But we don't have any proof," Ashley reminded her.

"You're right." Shannon paused. "I'm

sure Ms. Braun noticed that the cheers were alike. But she will want proof before we accuse the Pirates of stealing them."

"Ashley and I can help with that," I said. "We're detectives."

Jessica's brown eyes widened in surprise. "You're kidding!"

"No, she's not," Ashley said with a smile. "We've solved loads of cases."

"Awesome!" Jenna cried. "But can you solve this mystery before we lose *all* the contests in the Cheerlympics?" She sounded worried.

"Don't worry," I assured the squad. "The Trenchcoat Twins are on the case. Starting right now!"

# ON THE CASE

"**L**et's talk to Patty first," I said, as the counselors announced an ice-cream break. Most of our squad gathered around the coolers, while Jessica jogged off toward the dorm.

Ashley and I each got a Popsicle, and then we headed across the field, looking for Patty. "Good idea," she said. "Patty said she wrote the cheer for the Best Cheer contest. But writing a cheer just doesn't seem like something Patty would want to do."

"I agree!" I said. "She always gripes when we have to write a report for school."

Ashley took her detective notebook out of her gym bag. She carries that notebook with her everywhere. She's very organized!

"Patty goes onto our suspect list." Ashley quickly wrote Patty's name in her notebook. Then she wrote the word *motive*. A motive is a reason for doing something. "Why would Patty steal our cheers?" she asked.

"Because she always wants to win, no matter what," I said. "*And* she hates to write."

"True." Ashley wrote Patty's motives in her notebook. Then she pointed toward a picnic table next to the field. "There are the Pirates. But I don't see Patty with them."

"She has to be here somewhere." I looked all around the field. Where was she?

I glanced across the grassy square to our dorm. A girl with a brown ponytail was coming out the door.

*Is that Patty?* I wondered. *Why would she be in our dorm?*

I was wrong. It was Jessica, not Patty. She walked across the square back toward the field.

A moment later another girl with a brown ponytail came out of our dorm. This time it *was* Patty!

"There she is!" I said, pointing.

Patty glanced from side to side as if she didn't want anyone to see her. Then she hurried over toward her squad.

Ashley looked at me. "What was Patty doing in our dorm?"

"And why did she look so sneaky?" I wondered. "Let's go talk to her!"

We hurried to catch up to Patty. I was about to call her name when someone shouted *our* names!

"Mary-Kate! Ashley! Wait a moment!"

A girl with short sandy hair and lots of freckles was coming out of the dorm. It was Haley Dawson. She's a CIT at Camp Pom-Pom this summer, like Shannon, but she can't cheer or coach because she hurt her knee.

"I just put in a new roll of film, and I want to get a picture of all the Eagles together," Haley said, holding up a shiny silver camera. She limped a little as she walked toward us.

Haley's seriously into photography, so both camps made her the official Cheer-lympics photographer. She took our official squad photo, and it's great. We hung it in the practice room, and everybody signed it.

"Would you guys pose for me?" Haley asked.

I glanced toward the road. The Camp Spirit bus wasn't there yet to pick up the Pirates. "We have to talk to someone," I said.

"I'll be super fast," Haley promised.

Ashley waved her arms and shouted for our squad to join us.

I pointed to Haley's camera. "What's that blue thing on the side?"

Haley held the camera toward me. "It's a sticker of a dolphin. I think dolphins are amazing."

"Oh," I said. I looked toward the Pirates again. They were still there, but their bus might come any minute now!

"Did you know that dolphins can talk to each other?" Haley added. "And I love how they leap into the air. I put dolphin stickers on all my equipment."

The rest of our squad ran up. "Why don't you do a cheer move so I can get a nice action shot?" Haley suggested.

"Spread eagle!" Ashley said quickly, looking toward the field again. "One . . . two . . . three!"

"Say *cheer*!" Haley cried as we all leaped up at once.

"Cheer!" we shouted.

As soon as Haley snapped the picture,

Ashley and I took off running. We skidded to a stop in front of Patty. "Patty, can we talk to you?" Ashley asked.

Patty shrugged. "Okay. But I already know what you want to talk about," she said.

"You do?" I asked. *Whoa*, I thought. *Is she going to confess?*

Patty nodded. "You want to congratulate us on winning the Best Spirit contest! We're going to win the whole Cheerlympics," she added. "The trophy will look great on my dresser."

"Your Spirit cheer *was* great," Ashley told her. "So was the one you did yesterday. The words *and* the moves."

I jumped in. "They were so great, we wanted to ask where you got them," I said.

Patty frowned. "What do you mean? I didn't *get* them anywhere. I made up the routines myself."

"Did anybody help you?" I asked.

"No!" Patty declared, crossing her arms. "They were *all* my ideas. Just ask my squad."

The other Pirates nodded. "It's true," one of them told us. "Patty came up with the routines and taught them to us."

"See?" Patty said. She glared at us.

"Why are you asking, anyway?" another girl wanted to know.

"We were just curious." I decided to change the subject fast. "Hey, Patty, do you ever miss Camp Pom-Pom?" I wanted to find out why she'd been inside our dorm.

"No way," Patty said. "Camp Spirit is much more my style. It even has an Olympic pool! Why would I miss Camp Pom-Pom and that dinky little lake?"

"Well, we saw you coming out of our dorm a little while ago," Ashley told her.

Patty frowned. "I went to the dorm to use the phone," she said. "Do you have a problem with that?"

"No," I said. "Of course not." I wondered if she was telling the truth.

"Good," she huffed. She stormed away.

Ashley and I headed back across the field. "Did you believe Patty?" I asked.

"I don't know," Ashley said. "She *could* have been making a phone call."

"Maybe Jessica saw her," I said. "She came out of the dorm right before Patty, remember?"

"We'll ask her," Ashley said. "But, Mary-Kate, what I can't figure out is *how* Patty could steal our routines. She would have to actually watch us do them, and she's hardly ever here."

I suddenly stopped walking. "What if Patty doesn't have to watch us?" I said. "What if someone is telling her all about them? Someone right here at our own camp!"

Ashley's eyes widened. "Maybe even on our own squad!"

# IS THE TATTLETALE AN EAGLE?

**A**shley and I stared at each other. "Jessica!" we said together.

"She and Patty were in our dorm at the same time," I said. "And Jessica really wanted to be captain. What if she's so mad, she's giving Patty our routines to make you look bad?"

Ashley frowned. "Jessica is one of us. I hope you're wrong. But we have to check it out." She took out her detective notebook and wrote down Jessica's name and motive.

"We need to talk to her," I said. I looked around the field. Jessica was sitting by herself on the bleachers. She looked like she was writing a letter.

We hurried over to her.

"Hi, Jessica!" I said. "We need to ask you something. Did you see Patty O'Leary in the dorm when you went back there after the contest?"

Jessica looked surprised. "Why would Patty be in our dorm?"

"We don't know for sure," Ashley said. "But we saw Patty come out right after you."

"Well, *I* didn't see her," Jessica said. "Nobody was downstairs when I left."

"Why did you go to the dorm?" I asked.

"I had to make a phone call," Jessica said. Her face turned red. She turned back to her letter, ignoring us.

"Uh, okay," I said. "See you later." She looked like she wasn't going to answer any more questions.

"I'm surprised she didn't see Patty," I said to Ashley as we walked away. "The phones are in all in the common area."

Ashley shrugged. "If Jessica is giving our secrets to Patty, she wouldn't admit she saw Patty. But we can't accuse her without any proof."

"That's true." I sighed. "Too bad there's no way to find out if Patty really made a phone call . . . *or* if Jessica did either."

"So now we have two suspects," Ashley said. "And no proof!"

"We have to solve this case before someone steals our next two cheers!" I cried.

"Let's warm up!" Shannon called out in the practice room the next morning. "Leg lifts, then side high kicks!"

Shannon turned on a boom box. We always do our warm-ups to music because it gives us more pep. But nobody had much pep this morning.

"You guys are so droopy!" Shannon said, running her fingers through her short blond hair. "Let's see some bounce!"

"It's hard to be bouncy when we're losing," Nicole complained.

"The game isn't over yet," Shannon reminded us. "If you want to win, let's see some winning spirit!"

I knew she was right. But it was hard to concentrate on anything but the case!

"Go, Eagles!" Shannon cheered.

"Go, Eagles!" we shouted back.

"I can't hear you!" Shannon called out.

"Go, Eagles!" we shouted again, a lot louder.

"That's more like it!" She smiled at us, and we bounced through the rest of our warm-ups. Then it was time to practice our Liberty. The third contest, Best Stunt, was tonight, and we wanted to win this one!

In a Liberty one cheerleader is called the flyer. Most of the others are the bases. They take hold of the flyer's ankles and lift her in a standing position above their heads. It's as if she's standing on air!

I'm the flyer in our Liberty. Heights used to terrify me, but I'm getting better. Now they just scare me!

Ashley led us in the cheer.

*"We're going to the top!*

*Going straight to the top!*

*Going up, going up, going up!"*

Jenna, Jessica, Nicole, and Risa grabbed my ankles and lifted me into the air. Ashley, Christy, and Shannon formed a circle around us. They were the spotters. They would catch me if I fell.

*Lock your legs,* I told myself as I went up. *Arms out. Eyes straight ahead.*

I stared across the room toward the window. Kayla Majors was peeking in at us. "Whoa!" I gasped.

"Are you okay, Mary-Kate?" Ashley asked.

"No!" I said. "I mean, yes! Get me down!"

As soon as my feet hit the floor, I ran to the window. But Kayla was gone.

"Mary-Kate, what's wrong?" Shannon asked.

"Uh . . . nothing. I'm sorry," I said. As we started practicing again, I whispered to Ashley, "I just saw Kayla spying on us!"

Her eyes widened.

When it was time for a break, Ashley and I walked across the grassy square toward the dorm, while the others went for a swim in the lake.

"Kayla's stepsister, Tara, is on the Pirates," Ashley said. "Maybe Kayla is trying to help them win."

"She could be upset that her squad, the Bears, wasn't chosen to represent Camp Pom-Pom," I added.

Ashley nodded. "So she spies on us, memorizes our routines, and then tells Tara and Patty about them."

I sighed. "I really like Kayla," I said.

"I do too," Ashley said. "But we have to put her on the suspect list."

Ashley wrote Kayla's name in her notebook. "You know what we need?" she asked. "Evidence. We have suspects and motives but no evidence!"

I grabbed Ashley's arm and pulled her behind some bushes. "We might have some evidence now!" I whispered. "Check it out!"

We both peered over the tops of the bushes. Kayla ran by, carrying a thick envelope under one arm.

"That envelope is stuffed full of something!" I whispered.

"Maybe drawings of our routines!" Ashley whispered back. "And the words to all our cheers!"

"Let's see where she's going!" I said. We hurried out from behind the bushes and ran down the walk. When we got to the back of the dorm, no one was there.

"Where did she go?" I asked.

Ashley shrugged. "Let's keep looking."

The dining hall was the next building. A white truck was parked near the back door.

I sniffed. "Pizza for lunch."

Ashley giggled. "Good detective work."

"Now if I could just sniff out Kayla," I said.

Ashley held up her hand. "Listen!" she whispered.

Voices were coming from inside the kitchen. One of them was Kayla's. "I was afraid I missed you!" she said. "And this is so important!"

"She's coming this way. We can't let her see us!" I glanced around. One of the truck's back doors was partly open. "Quick, into the truck!"

Ashley and I jumped up and tumbled through the open truck door. *Wham!* I rolled up against a wooden crate. *Thump!* A fat green cabbage plopped into my lap. *Slam!* The truck door closed.

I blinked in the dim light. Stacked

around us were crates of carrots, broccoli, onions, and cabbage. "We're surrounded," I whispered, "by vegetables."

"At least we won't starve," Ashley whispered back.

Kayla's voice was louder now. She must be right next to the truck! I clutched the cabbage and leaned toward the door.

"You know my stepsister, Tara, don't you?" Kayla asked.

"I sure do," a woman's voice replied. "Do you want me to give her something again?"

*Again?* My eyebrows shot up.

"Another envelope," Kayla said. There was a crinkling noise. "Thank you! It's really, really important!"

"No problem," the woman said.

I stared at Ashley. Her eyebrows were up as far as mine. Had we actually solved the case?

*Vroom! Vroom!* The truck suddenly rumbled and shook. It was about to drive off— with Ashley and me inside!

# 5

# CLOSE CALL

"**A**hhh!" Ashley and I screamed at the same time. We quickly jumped out before the truck moved.

The driver hopped out and rushed back to us. "What's going on? Who was screaming?" She frowned at me. "And what are you doing with that cabbage?"

Uh-oh. I was still holding it! I quickly put it back into the truck. "Sorry," I said. "I forgot I had it."

The woman's frown got deeper. "Were

you two in my truck?" she demanded. "I deliver vegetables to this camp and Camp Spirit. Vegetables, not stowaways."

"We aren't stowaways," Ashley told her. "We were . . . um . . . "

"Checking out the veggies," I piped up. "But mostly we were looking for somebody. A girl with red hair. I think she gave you an envelope to take to her stepsister at Camp Spirit."

"She did," the woman said. "But you won't find her in the back of my truck."

"You're right! She's not there!" I said with a big smile. "We'll look for her somewhere else."

Ashley and I hurried away. "We have to tell Kayla we know what she's doing," I said.

Ashley shook her head. "We don't have enough evidence yet. We don't actually know what was in that envelope."

I sighed. I was itching to jump into things—but it was still too soon!

"Don't worry, Mary-Kate. If Kayla's stealing our cheers, we'll catch her," Ashley promised.

Ashley and I checked the lakefront, the dorm, and even the dining hall again for Kayla. No luck.

"I'm thirsty," Ashley said as we neared the recreation room. "I need a soda."

"Good idea," I said.

We jogged to the recreation room. It has vending machines, a Ping-Pong table, books and magazines, and lots of comfortable chairs and couches.

Kayla was sitting on one of the couches.

Ashley and I ducked behind the door before she saw us.

"What's she doing?" Ashley whispered.

I peered around the door. "Reading a magazine," I reported. "Oops!" I quickly ducked back. "She almost saw me!"

I counted to three and then peeked out again. Ashley peered over my shoulder.

Kayla slipped a pair of scissors from her pocket. She quickly cut a page from the magazine. The she picked up another magazine. *Snip, snip, snip* went the scissors again.

I glanced at Ashley. She nodded. We strolled into the room together. We pretended not to see Kayla at first.

"I am *so* thirsty!" I said. I watched Kayla out of the corner of my eye as I fed some quarters into a vending machine.

Kayla quickly slipped the scissors and cutouts behind her. Then she grabbed another magazine and flipped it open.

Ashley bought a can of Sparkling Strawberry and turned around. "Oh, hi, Kayla!" she said.

"Hi." Kayla's face turned red.

I sipped my Mango Madness. "Hey, Kayla. How come your magazine's upside down?"

Kayla lowered the magazine and grinned. "I guess you caught me!"

*Yes!* I thought. *But wait—if we caught her, why is she smiling?*

"I found some more great pictures!" Kayla lowered her voice and waved the magazine at us. "I just had to have them for my scrapbook, so I cut them out."

I suddenly got it. "Pictures of Justin DiNardo?" I asked.

"Who else?" Kayla giggled. "But don't tell anybody, okay? I probably shouldn't be cutting up the camp's magazines. But I can't help it. I just love pictures of Justin!"

"Is that what you sent to Tara—pictures?" Ashley asked.

"We heard you talking to the vegetable lady," I explained.

Kayla nodded. "We both keep Justin scrapbooks. We trade pictures. Now I have some new ones for her!"

Kayla stood up. She grabbed the cutouts and her scissors. "See you guys later. And please, *please* don't tell anybody about the magazines!" she said. She left the room.

"I guess Kayla was sending pictures to Tara, not cheers," I said.

"We don't know that for sure," Ashley said. "She could have sent other stuff too—like descriptions of our routines. We can't take her off our suspect list yet. Who knows how many times she's watched us practice?"

Suddenly I thought of something terrible. "The Stunt contest is tonight!" I wailed. "What if the thief already gave our stunt routine to the Pirates?"

"Let them do it, Mary-Kate!" Ashley grinned at me. "I have a plan that will give the Pirates a major surprise!"

# 6

# THE BIG SWITCH

**I** had to wait to hear about Ashley's plan. As soon as we returned to the practice room, she hurried over to talk to Shannon. The rest of the squad rushed over to *me*.

"Have you solved the case yet?" Jenna asked. "Do you know who did it?"

"I bet it was Patty O'Leary," Nicole said. "Did you talk to her?"

I nodded. "But we don't know anything for sure yet."

"What *do* you know?" Jessica demanded.

"It's too soon to say," I replied. I couldn't let Jessica know she was one of our suspects. "The number one detective rule is, Don't talk about your cases. You might say something to tip off a suspect."

Shannon clapped her hands. "Listen up, everybody. Ashley just came up with a great idea. We're not going to do the Liberty."

Jessica's mouth fell open. "What?"

The rest of the squad looked confused. I was a little confused myself!

"We can't do a Stunt cheer without a stunt!" Jessica protested.

Ashley smiled. "Don't worry, we'll do a stunt. Just not the Liberty."

"Right," Shannon said. "We'll do the Pyramid you learned last week. It's fantastic!"

"Oh, I get it!" I said. "The Pirates won't have time to steal it before the contest tonight!"

"And the Liberty is totally boring next to the Pyramid!" Risa said, grinning.

"Only if we do it well," Jessica argued. "The Pyramid is really hard. We haven't practiced it enough!"

"Sure, we have," Shannon told her. "And we're going to practice it some more right now."

Jessica looked really upset. *Who is she worried about?* I wondered. *The Eagles? Or the Pirates?*

"Don't worry, Jessica. The Pyramid is a very impressive stunt," Shannon told her. "The judges are going to love it! Mary-Kate, are you up for it?"

I'm the flyer, the one on top of the Pyramid. I knew I would be scared. But if it would help my squad, I was definitely up for it!

"Let's do it!" I cried. "Let's go, Eagles!"

A few hours later I shivered with excitement. We were all in the gym at Camp Spirit.

The bleachers were full. The Best Stunt contest was about to start!

"The Pirates have won the coin toss!" the judge declared. "Pirates, please begin!"

"They have all the luck," Jenna grumbled. "They keep winning the coin toss."

"We don't have to worry this time," I reminded her. "There's no way they can do our routine!"

Patty and her squad ran into the middle of the gym.

"*Here we go! Watch us go!*" the Pirates shouted. "*Going up! Going up! Going up!*"

Four of the Pirates lifted Patty up into the air.

"They're doing the Liberty!" I cried. "You were right, Ashley—they didn't have time to change their stunt!"

"We'll beat them for sure with the Pyramid," Risa said.

The Pirates finished and ran to their side of the gym.

"Eagles, you may begin," the judge called out.

Shannon gave us all a big smile. "You're going to be great! Remember to have fun. Go, Eagles!"

My heart pounded as we ran onto the floor. I wasn't thinking about the Pirates anymore. I just wanted to do my best!

*"We are the Eagles!*
*We're gonna fly, fly, fly!"*

The crowd in the bleachers clapped and cheered as we all did a flying split. Then it was time for the Pyramid.

*"We're rising high, high, high!"* we chanted. *"We'll touch the sky, sky, sky!"*

Jessica, Ashley, and Nicole formed the bottom of the pyramid. Shannon helped Risa and Christy climb onto their shoulders. Then it was my turn.

Shannon helped me climb up. I put one foot on Risa's shoulder, the other on Christy's.

I took a deep breath. I stood up straight and held my arms out from my sides. *Don't wobble!* I told myself. *Eyes forward! Smile!*

I slowly stretched one leg up behind me—and smiled! I really did feel as if I could fly!

People were clapping and shouting. The crowd went wild as we finished our cheer. I felt great! Now all I had to do was get down!

I bent my knees and did a pike jump, touching my toes in midair, then straightening my legs. I landed neatly on my feet. *Phew!*

The crowd whistled and stomped and cheered. I couldn't stop smiling. *We did it!* I thought. Even the judges were smiling.

"You guys were *so* good!" Shannon cried. She gave us all high fives.

The dark-haired judge walked slowly into the middle of the gym. *Walk faster!* I thought. I couldn't wait to hear the results.

"Once again, both squads were great," the judge said with a smile. "This time, first place goes to . . ."

*Say "The Eagles!"* I thought.

"The Eagles, with nine points!" the judge announced. "The Pirates are second, with six."

"All right!" I shouted. I hugged Ashley. Ashley hugged me. Everyone on the squad jumped up and down and hugged one another.

Haley Dawson came over and snapped a picture of our group hug. "You guys were great!" she said. "I really miss cheering since I hurt my knee. Especially in the Cheerlympics."

"I bet," I said. "What squad were you on?"

"The Sharks." Haley smiled. "Every year." She snapped a few more pictures and then headed out to the bus with us.

When we got back to Camp Pom-Pom, Ashley and I went to our room. We changed out of our uniforms into shorts and T-shirts. Then we went to the recreation room to get a snack—and to talk about the case.

Ashley plopped down onto a couch and took out her detective notebook. "What do we know so far?"

"We don't *know* anything!" I sat next to her and ripped open a bag of trail mix.

In front of us was the table with Kayla's favorite fan magazines scattered all over the top. While we talked, Ashley started putting them into a pile. She's extremely organized!

I popped an almond into my mouth and closed my eyes. *Think!* I told myself.

"Mary-Kate!" Ashley gasped.

My eyes popped open.

"Look what just fell out of this magazine!" Ashley was holding a spiral notebook.

She flipped through the notebook's pages. They were filled with notes and diagrams—of the Eagles' routines!

# 7

# TAKE NOTE

"**Q**uick, Ashley, see if there's a name on it!" I cried. "This could be our big break!"

Ashley checked the front and back of the notebook. She flipped through all the pages. "No name," she said. "But check out the handwriting."

I scanned the pages. "It slants to the left. And there are little hearts over the *i*'s."

"And the ink is all the same color—neon orange," Ashley added.

"Do you think this is Kayla's notebook?"

I asked. "Maybe she left it here by accident."

"We need to see her handwriting," Ashley said. "Jessica's too."

I popped another almond into my mouth and chewed slowly. "Our squad poster!" I said. "We all signed it, remember? Kayla isn't on our squad, so her handwriting won't be on it, but Jessica's will."

"Good thinking, Mary-Kate." Ashley jumped up. "Let's take a look!"

We hurried to the practice room, where our squad poster hung. We quickly scanned the signatures.

"There!" I said. I pointed to a name written in bright orange ink. It slanted to the left. And it had little hearts over the *i*'s.

"Jessica Kim!" Ashley groaned. "I really didn't want it to be Jessica!"

I felt the same way. I knew Jessica was jealous because Ashley was made captain. But she's still part of our squad!

I shook my head. "I don't understand how

she could give our routines to the Pirates."

Ashley looked *so* disappointed. "I don't know," she said. "We'll have to ask her."

We found Jessica running laps around the field. We waved, and she trotted over to us.

"What's up?" she puffed, jogging in place. Her face was red from running. "I have three more laps to do."

"This won't take long." Ashley handed her the notebook. "This is yours, isn't it?"

Jessica looked at it. "Yes, it's mine. Where did you get it?"

"From the recreation room," I said. "You shouldn't have left it lying around. Someone could use it to give our routines to the Pirates."

"I guess you're right," Jessica agreed.

"Why did you write down all our routines, anyway?" Ashley asked.

"So I wouldn't forget anything," Jessica explained. "I want to get really, really good this summer and make squad captain next year. I practice alone a lot, and I use my notebook to help me remember all the moves."

"That makes sense," I said to Ashley.

Jessica's eyes widened. "Wait—you don't think *I'm* giving our routines away, do you?" she asked. "I would never do that."

"Well . . . " I began.

Jessica cut me off. "If I was giving the Pirates our routines, my notebook would be at Camp Spirit, not here!"

"We're not accusing you of anything," Ashley said quickly.

"That's good." Jessica spun around and jogged away.

"I don't know if I believe her or not," Ashley said, watching her. Then she turned to me. "But I just thought of something. How would Jessica get her notebook to Camp Spirit? It's not like she can go back and forth between camps every day."

"You're right, Ashley," I said. "Maybe Jessica can't—but I know someone who can!"

# 8

# ANOTHER SUSPECT!

"**H**aley Dawson goes to both camps to take pictures!" I said. "She could be taking pictures of our routines and showing them to the Pirates!"

"But we would have noticed if she took pictures of our practices," Ashley said. "Besides, what is Haley's motive? She's not even in the Cheerlympics."

Ashley had a point. Two points. But I had a hunch, and I couldn't let it go. "What are the rules about leaving camp?" I asked.

"The first day we were here, they said we had to sign out if we wanted to leave," Ashley reminded me. "There's a sign-out book in the office."

The office was closed for the night. "We'll get up extra early tomorrow and check," Ashley said as we walked back to the dorm.

"Right," I yawned. "How 'extra'?"

Ashley laughed. "'Extra' enough to catch a cheer-thief, I hope!"

The next morning, my stomach gave an extra-loud growl on the way to the camp office, but I wanted to follow my hunch first. We had just one day left to solve this case before the Cheerlympics was over, with the Best Dance contest tomorrow morning. Breakfast would have to wait!

The office had shelves and shelves of yearbooks and cheerleading manuals. The secretary, Ms. Wilcox, was behind her desk working at the computer. She smiled at us over the monitor. "Can I help you?"

"Could we please see the sign-out book?" I asked.

"Sure." She slid a big three-ring notebook across the desk.

The phone rang. Ms. Wilcox picked it up, tucking her brown hair behind one ear. While she talked, I flipped open the notebook. Ashley peered over my shoulder while I ran a finger down the list of names.

"There's Haley's name!" I whispered. "And there it is again! Ashley, look at the times she leaves Camp Pom-Pom!"

"Every day—right after our practices are over!" Ashley whispered. "You may be right, Mary-Kate!"

As I started to close the book, I suddenly noticed another name. And this one was written in neon-orange ink! "Jessica has been leaving the camp too! Lots of times!"

Ashley groaned. "So she's still a suspect."

We waved good-bye to Ms. Wilcox and hurried out of the office. We passed the dining hall.

I took a deep sniff. "Apple-cinnamon muffins—I'm sure of it!" I said as my stomach growled again.

"Okay, you talked me into it." Ashley laughed. "Let's eat. Then we'll ask Jessica why she's always leaving the camp."

Most of our squad was in the dining hall. Ashley and I got muffins and juice and sat down across the table from Jessica.

"I might have to leave camp for a little while today," Jessica said. "Don't worry, though. I won't miss practice."

"You leave camp a lot, don't you?" Ashley asked. "Mary-Kate and I noticed your name in the sign-out book."

I tried to see if Jessica looked guilty, but she just looked embarrassed!

"I've been visiting my parents," she said quietly. "I call home a lot too."

"Oh! Is that why you went back to the dorm after the Best Spirit contest? To call home?" I asked.

"Yes," Jessica admitted. "This is my first time at sleep-away camp. I like it, but sometimes I get homesick."

Ashley and I finished our muffins and headed to practice. "Do you believe Jessica?" I asked.

"She looked like she was telling the truth," Ashley said. "But she could stop off at Camp Spirit when she goes to visit her parents."

"What about Haley?" I asked.

"She's a good suspect too. She has a camera, and she leaves camp after all our practices. But she doesn't have a motive, like Jessica does," Ashley said, frustrated. "I say we keep them both on the suspect list."

"And don't forget Kayla and Patty," I reminded my sister. "If only we could find some proof!"

We got to the practice room and helped set up. I picked up a chair from the middle of the room so Shannon could lay out the exercise mats. A bunch of little white flakes were on the floor around the chair.

I picked one up and rubbed it between my fingers. *Paint flakes,* I realized. *Where had they come from?*

*Tweeet!* Shannon blew her whistle. "Let's get started!" She turned on her boom box.

Our Dance routine is really cute. We wear top hats and start with a kick line. We toss the top hats down and dance a funky hip-hop around them while we cheer. Then we pick up the top hats and finish with another kick line.

"That's looking great!" Shannon said after we went through the routine three times. She checked her watch. "Okay, take a break. Meet back here in half an hour!"

As the rest of the squad left, Shannon

turned to Ashley and me. "How is the case going?"

"We're still working on it," I told her.

"Maybe we should add something to the Dance routine," Ashley told Shannon. "We really need to wow those judges tomorrow."

"Sure!" Shannon replied. "I have to go to a CIT meeting right now. We'll put our heads together after the break."

Ashley and I left the practice room. "Do you mind if we go back to the office?" Ashley asked. "I want to look at yearbook pictures of other Cheerlympics for ideas for our routine."

"Sounds like fun," I said.

We hurried back to the office. Ms. Wilcox wasn't there. But anybody could look at the yearbooks. We grabbed a pile and sat on the floor with them.

I pointed to an old picture of the Tigers squad. "The Tigers used straw hats and canes in their Dance routine. What if we did something with canes?"

"Canes could be fun," Ashley said, flipping through some pages. "Or maybe something tricky with our hats. The Bears are twirling cowboy hats over their heads."

Ashley turned to the back of the yearbook. "Here's a list of winners for the last five years. Whoa! The Pirates have almost always lost to a Camp Pom-Pom squad!"

"Of course," I grinned. "We're the best of the best!"

Ashley gasped. "Mary-Kate, check out this picture!"

I peered at the page. It had two photos on it. One was of the winning squad from Camp Pom-Pom. The other was of the second-place squad from Camp Spirit, the Pirates.

Ashley pointed to a girl on the Pirates squad. A girl with short sandy hair and lots of freckles.

"It's Haley Dawson!" I exclaimed. "Haley wasn't a Shark. She was a Pirate! She lied to us!"

# A CLUE IN THE CEILING

**A**shley and I stared at the photo of Haley on the Pirates squad. "She definitely kept this a secret," Ashley said.

"Because she's been stealing our routines for her old team!" I declared.

"We can't jump to conclusions," Ashley said. "We have to ask Haley why she told us she was on the Sharks. But *first*," she added, "we have to figure out what to add to our Dance routine. The contest is tomorrow!"

We flipped through the yearbook again.

"That picture of the Bears waving their cowboy hats gave me an idea," Ashley said. "First we do a split. When we land, we toss our top hats into the air. We jump up, catch the hats on their way down, and put them back on. We could do it before the last kick line."

"Sounds great!" I said. "Let's try it. We'll worry about clues later."

We hurried back to the practice room. We put on our top hats and started. The timing was tricky. We both missed catching our hats.

After a couple of tries Ashley finally did it perfectly. "Try it again, Mary-Kate!" she said, tapping her hat onto her head. "Just remember to toss the hat way, *way* up."

I picked up my top hat and started the new move again. I tossed up my hat and stared at the ceiling.

"What is that?" I cried.

"It's your hat!" Ashley said. "Catch it!"

"No, *that*!" I said. I pointed to the ceiling

as my hat bounced off my right shoulder. "That blinking red light. See?"

Ashley came over and looked up with me.

One of the panels in the ceiling was crooked, leaving a little gap. Through it we saw a small red light blinking on and off.

I suddenly remembered something. "When I moved the chair before practice this morning I found paint flakes on the floor," I told Ashley. "In this exact spot. I wondered where they came from."

"Somebody moved that panel to put something in the ceiling," she said. "That must be how the paint chipped off. What has a blinking light like that?"

"I can think of *one* thing." I quickly got the chair and unfolded it. Ashley held it steady while I climbed onto it. I reached up to the panel and gave it a push.

"It's exactly what I thought!" I said. "A video camera! Somebody has been taping our practices!"

# 10

# CAUGHT ON TAPE

I stood on tiptoe and pulled the camera down through the gap. "Case closed, Ashley!"

"What do you mean?"

I pointed to the side of the camera.

"A dolphin sticker!" Ashley cried. "That camera belongs to Haley! She told us she puts dolphins on all her equipment!"

I pushed REWIND, then PLAY. We both peered into the viewfinder.

On the tape our squad marched across

the room. We held our top hats over our heads.

*"We're the high-flying Eagles!*
*The high-stepping Eagles!"*

I watched myself kick my right leg up just a little later than everybody else. "It's our practice from this morning," I said. "My timing was off."

"But your detective work is right on!" Ashley said. She turned the camera off. "We've got our proof. Now we can tell Ms. Braun."

As Ashley and I hurried out, we ran into the rest of our squad.

"Where are you going?" Jenna asked, twirling an orange Frisbee on one finger. "Isn't it time to practice?"

"We have to talk to Ms. Braun," I said. "It's really important."

"It's about the case, isn't it?" Christy asked. "Did you solve it?"

"We'll tell you later—promise," Ashley

said. She smiled at Jessica. "Jessica, would you be captain until I get back?"

Jessica's face lit up. "Sure!"

Ashley and I took off running. "I think you just cured Jessica's homesickness," I said.

Ashley giggled. "She was pretty surprised. But she's a good cheerleader. And I bet she'll make a good captain."

"Hey, what's the rush?" Shannon asked as she walked out of the staff building.

"We solved the case!" I said. "Come on! We'll explain everything to you and Ms. Braun together."

Ms. Braun was in her office. She smiled when she saw us. Then we showed her the videotape. By the time we finished telling her about Haley, the smile was gone.

"This is very serious," Ms. Braun said. She left her office for a few minutes. When she came back, Haley Dawson was with her. "Go ahead, Mary-Kate and Ashley," she said. "Tell Haley what you found in the practice room."

I held up the video camera. "We know this is yours. It has a dolphin sticker on it."

"And it has a tape of our practice *in* it," Ashley said. "You taped our routines for the Pirates, didn't you?"

At first Haley looked shocked. Then she looked sad. "Yes," she admitted. "I'm sorry! This is my last year at camp, and I *really* wanted my old squad—the Pirates—to win the Cheerlympics. But once I saw you guys, I knew you were just too good!"

"So you made the tapes and then gave them to Patty," I said.

Haley nodded. "Yes. I mean, no! I mean . . . I watched the tapes by myself, and then I taught the routines to Patty. But she didn't know I stole them. Then she taught the words and moves to the Pirates."

"Did the other girls on the team know the routines weren't Patty's?" Shannon asked.

Haley shook her head. "No way! Patty pretended she made them up herself."

Ashley and I glanced at each other. I could tell we were thinking the same thing: *Princess Patty always wants all the credit!*

"I'm really, really sorry," Haley said. "I know I shouldn't have done it."

Ms. Braun looked at Haley. "I think you need to find some way to make it up to the Eagles," she said sternly.

"I could take special portrait photos for each of the Eagles," Haley offered.

"Cool!" I said.

"That would be a start," said Ms. Braun. Then she turned to Ashley and me. "As for Patty, she didn't know the cheers were stolen, but she did try to pass off someone else's work as her own. This is serious enough to disqualify the Pirates."

"You mean they would be out of the Cheerlympics?" Ashley asked.

"Yes," Ms. Braun said.

Ashley and I looked at each other again. "But that wouldn't be any fun," I said. "And fun is what cheering is all about, right Shannon?"

Shannon smiled at me. "Right!"

"Besides, the rest of the Pirates didn't know they weren't Patty's routines," Ashley said.

"Well, the Pirates will have to come up with a new routine for the Best Dance contest tomorrow." Ms. Braun smiled at Ashley and me. "But the Cheerlympics will go on!"

"Five minutes, everybody!" Shannon said to the squad the next day on the field at Camp Pom-Pom. "Are you ready to rock?"

"And roll!" I shouted.

We all laughed. We had finally won the coin toss. It was almost time to do our Dance routine.

At first the other Eagles were angry when they found out about Haley and

Patty. But they wanted the Cheerlympics to go on too. Now we were all excited!

I was still a little worried about my kicking. I pulled Ashley away from the group.

"Tell me if my timing is okay," I said. I started chanting under my breath. "'We're the high-flying Eagles! The high-stepping Eagles!' Step, step, kick!"

"Good, Mary-Kate," Ashley told me.

"Really good," somebody else said.

I whirled around. "Patty!"

"Hi," Patty said. She looked at her feet. Then she looked directly at Ashley and me. "I'm sorry about what I did," she said. "I told everybody I could write great cheers, but it was way harder than I thought!"

"It isn't easy," Ashley agreed.

"I just knew that if my squad found out I couldn't write cheers, they would pick another captain," Patty said. "You probably don't believe me," she added, "but I really am sorry."

At that moment the dark-haired judge blew her whistle. It was time for the Best Dance contest to start!

*"We're the high-flying Eagles!*
*The high-stepping Eagles!"*

We ran onto the field and started our kick line. My timing was perfect!

We threw our top hats down and did our hip-hop around them. The crowd whistled and cheered. We grabbed our hats. Now it was time for Ashley's new move.

I leaped into a split and landed on the grass. I tossed my hat way, *way* up! I quickly jumped to my feet. My hat was tumbling toward the ground. I reached up—and caught it!

I took a quick glance at the others. *Yes!* We all caught our hats! We tapped them onto our heads and did our kick line off the field. The crowd went wild!

"That was amazing!" Shannon cried, giving us all a hug.

"And now, the Pirates!" the judge announced.

The Pirates ran onto the field.

*"Cheer for the Eagles!*
*We put them to the test!*
*Cheer for the Eagles!*
*They really are the best!"*

Ashley looked at me. "Did you hear that? They're cheering for *us*."

I grinned. "Patty *did* mean it when she said she was sorry. This cheer is proof!"

*"They're birds of a feather!"* the Pirates yelled, shaking their red pom-poms.

*"They've got it all together!*
*Cheer for the Eagles,*
*The best of the best!"*

After the Pirates ran off, the dark-haired judge reached for the microphone. "The Pirates scored eight points for that cheer," she declared. "And first place in the Best Dance contest goes to the Eagles, with ten points!"

We all jumped up and down and hugged one another.

The judge clapped her hands for attention. "And now I am pleased to announce this year's winner of the Cheerlympics. . . ."

I crossed my fingers for luck. I was so nervous!

"The Eagles!"

"We did it!" I screamed. We all high-fived. The Pirates all ran over and hugged us—even Patty! Haley snapped a gazillion pictures!

"And now let's have one big cheer from *all* the squads!" the judge called out.

"This is so much fun!" Ashley said as all the cheerleaders from both camps ran onto the field.

I turned a cartwheel and grinned. "That's what cheering is all about!"

Hi from both of us,

There were spooky sounds and strange lights coming from the evergreen maze. Our friend Mitch said it was haunted! Ashley and I didn't believe him . . . until we came face-to-face with a ghost!

Was the ghost real? Or was someone trying to scare us away? The only way to find out was to go back into the scary maze! Want to know what happened next? Check out the next page for a sneak peek at *The New Adventures of Mary-Kate & Ashley: The Case Of The Haunted Maze.*

See you next time!

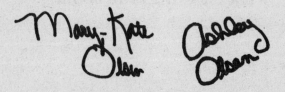

A sneak peek at our next mystery...

# The Case Of The

# HAUNTED MAZE

"Where is he?" I cried out. "Mitch! Mitch! Where are you?" Ashley and I were all alone in the evergreen maze now.

"He just disappeared," Ashley said. "But that's impossible. He must have taken one of those paths we passed."

I peered around a corner and almost choked. "Ashley—look!"

Through a gap in the hedges, two small glowing eyes peered back at us.

"Who . . . who are you?" I asked.

No answer.

As we stared at the eyes, they suddenly disappeared.

"Ghost eyes," I whispered. "Ashley—those were ghost eyes!"

*Thump . . . thump . . . thump.*

We both froze at the sound.

"What's *that*?" Ashley asked.

"I don't know," I said, "but we have to get out of here!"

Ashley didn't want to leave. "Wait," she said. "Don't you see what's going on? It's a prank! Mitch is trying to scare us! Let's find him and catch him in the act." Ashley closed her eyes and concentrated hard. "Listen—what direction is that sound coming from?" she asked.

We tried to follow the *thump, thump, thump* sounds but we couldn't find a path that led in the right direction. We searched on the ground for any signs of Mitch. I spotted the first clue.

"Footprints!" I said.

Sure enough, on a side path were clear marks shaped like sneakers. I felt calmer. Ghosts didn't wear sneakers, but Mitch did. We had something to follow.

Ashley took the lead, but I was right behind her. We could still hear that *thump, thump, thump* sound, and I wondered how Mitch was making that noise.

"Wait a minute," I said. "Now I see more footprints."

Ashley knelt down and examined them. "These are *our* footprints!" she said. "We're walking in circles."

"Let's go left," I said.

"No, I think we should go to the right," Ashley argued.

I couldn't help thinking about the girl in the ghost legend. We were lost, just like she was. And what if we couldn't find our way out either? One hundred years from now, would people still be talking about the twins who disappeared?

"Ashley! Mary-Kate!"

We whirled around.

It was Mitch, and his face was white.

*Thump . . . thump . . . thump.*

The thumping sounds grew louder and louder.

I wasn't making them.

And Ashley wasn't making them.

And Mitch wasn't making them.

So who was?

# Mary-Kate and Ashley

# Win an "Apple iPod®" Sweepstakes

*A PORTABLE DIGITAL MUSIC PLAYER!*

Record hours of music from your favorite CDs or online music sites! Load it up and carry it in your pocket!

# The New Adventures of Mary-Kate and Ashley
## Apple iPod® Sweepstakes
## OFFICIAL RULES:

**1. NO PURCHASE OR PAYMENT NECESSARY TO ENTER OR WIN.**

**2. How to Enter.** To enter, complete the official entry form or hand print your name, address, age and phone number along with the words "New Adventures Apple iPod® Sweepstakes" on a 3" x 5" card and mail to: New Adventures Apple iPod® Sweepstakes, c/o HarperEntertainment, Attn: Children's Marketing Department, 10 East 53rd Street, New York, NY 10022. Entries must be received no later than February 28, 2005. Enter as often as you wish, but each entry must be mailed separately. One entry per envelope. Partially completed, illegible, or mechanically reproduced entries will not be accepted. Sponsor are not responsible for lost, late, mutilated, illegible, stolen, postage due, incomplete or misdirected entries. All entries become the property of Dualstar Entertainment Group, LLC, and will not be returned.

**3. Eligibility.** Sweepstakes open to all legal residents of the United States (excluding Colorado and Rhode Island) who are between the ages of five and fifteen on February 28, 2005 excluding employees and immediate family members of HarperCollins Publishers, Inc., ("HarperCollins"), Parachute Properties and Parachute Press, Inc., and their respective subsidiaries and affiliates, officers, directors, shareholders, employees, agents, attorneys, and other representatives and their immediate families (individually and collectively, "Parachute"), Dualstar Entertainment Group, LLC, and its subsidiaries and affiliates, officers, directors, shareholders, employees, agents, attorneys, and other representatives and their immediate families (individually and collectively, "Dualstar"), and their respective parent companies, affiliates, subsidiaries, advertising, promotion and fulfillment agencies, and the persons with whom each of the above are domiciled. All applicable federal, state and local laws and regulations apply. Offer void where prohibited or restricted by law.

**4. Odds of Winning.** Odds of winning depend on the total number of entries received. Approximately 300,000 sweepstakes announcements published. All prizes will be awarded. Winner will be randomly drawn on or about March 15, 2005, by HarperCollins, whose decision is final. Potential winner will be notified by mail and will be required to sign and return an affidavit of eligibility and release of liability within 14 days of notification. Prizes won by minors will be awarded to parent or legal guardian who must sign and return all required legal documents. By acceptance of their prize, winners consent to the use of their names, photographs, likeness, and biographical information by HarperCollins, Parachute, Dualstar, and for publicity purposes without further compensation except where prohibited.

**5. Grand Prize.** One Grand Prize Winner will win an Apple iPod®. Approximate retail value of prize totals $500.00.

**6. Prize Limitations.** All prizes will be awarded. Only one prize will be awarded per individual, family, or household. Prizes are non-transferable and cannot be sold or redeemed for cash. No cash substitute is available. Any federal, state, or local taxes are the responsibility of the winner. Sponsor may substitute prize of equal or greater value, if necessary, due to availability.

**7. Additional terms:** By participating, entrants agree a) to the official rules and decisions of the judges, which will be final in all respects; and to waive any claim to ambiguity of the official rules and b) to release, discharge, and hold harmless HarperCollins, Parachute, Dualstar, and their respective parent companies, affiliates, subsidiaries, employees and representatives and advertising, promotion and fulfillment agencies from and against any and all liability or damages associated with acceptance, use, or misuse of any prize received or participation in any Sweepstakes-related activity or participation in this Sweepstakes.

**8. Dispute Resolution.** Any dispute arising from this Sweepstakes will be determined according to the laws of the State of New York, without reference to its conflict of law principles, and the entrants consent to the personal jurisdiction of the State and Federal courts located in New York County and agree that such courts have exclusive jurisdiction over all such disputes.

**9. Winner Information.** To obtain the name of the winner, please send your request and a self-addressed stamped envelope (residents of Vermont may omit return postage) to New Adventures Apple iPod® Sweepstakes Winner, c/o HarperEntertainment, 10 East 53rd Street, New York, NY 10022 after April 15, 2005, but no later than October 15, 2005.

**10. Sweepstakes Sponsor:** HarperCollins Publishers, Inc. Apple© Corporation is not affiliated, connected or associated with this Sweepstakes in any manner and bears no responsibility for the administration of this Sweepstakes.

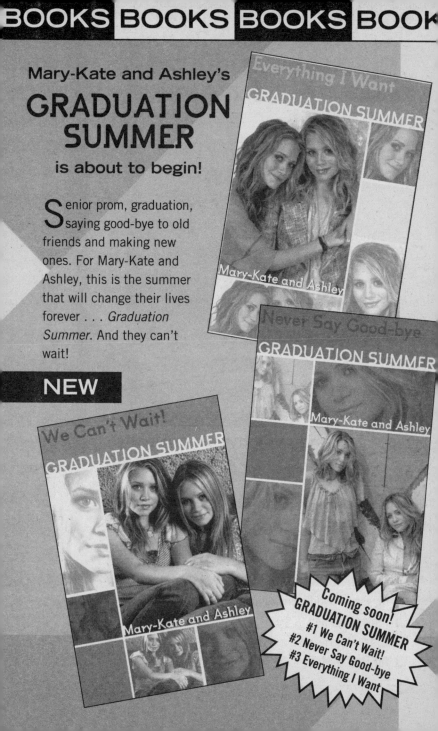

mary-kate olsen
ashley olsen
eugene levy
new york minute
In Theaters May 7th
www.newyorkminutemovie.com
WARNER BROS. PICTURES
©2004 Warner Bros. Ent. All Rights Reserved